THE WAY WE FALL

SHIRLEY SIATON

THE WAY WE FALL
Short Love Stories

ISBN 978-1-961052-25-3 (paperback)

1st Edition, November 2025

Published by Inky Sword Book Publishing
Cover design by Temptation Creations
Interior formatting by Champagne Book Design

Inky Sword Book Publishing
Barangay Quezon, Arevalo, Iloilo City 5000
Republic of the Philippines
inkysword.com

A NOTE FOR THE READER

These love stories are an exploration of connection, the magic of fleeting moments, and the profound ache of a 'what-if.' Each tale is a window into the many ways we fall—the paths that lead us home, the ones that lead us astray, and the ones that change us forever.

As in life, not all of these paths are easy, and not all falls end with a gentle landing. Not all stories in this collection have a conventionally happy ending (HEA). Some include breakups and themes of profound angst, regret, and ambiguous endings.

For your care and consideration, I wanted to provide a gentle heads-up on some of the heavier emotional themes you will encounter within these pages.

Please be aware that this collection includes:
- Grief following the death of a loved one from illness.
- Major character death.
- Discussions of eating disorders and malnutrition.
- References to chronic and terminal illnesses.
- Past infidelity and emotional/financial betrayal by a partner.
- Themes of parental abandonment, neglect, and past off-page abuse.

Thank you for opening your heart to *The Way We Fall*. Please read kindly and look after yourself.

For all those who believe in love

And those who refuse to stop believing

CONTENTS

THE WAY WE FALL

CHAPTER 1

WRONG NUMBER, RIGHT LOVE

THE FIRST TIME IT HAPPENS, I'M STILL AT THE OFFICE. It's a little past nine in the evening, and the fluorescent lights hum louder than my own pulse. The rest of the floor is empty, but I'm still here, squinting at spreadsheets for the president of the health services company where I work as his personal assistant.

My phone buzzes.

It's a strange number, one not on my extensive contacts list.

I pick up without thinking. "Yes, hello?"

There's a pause. Then a male voice, low and slightly panicked, says, *"Wait. This isn't Paolo?"*

"No," I answer, frowning at the glowing monitor. "This is Edna."

"Oh. Uh…sorry. Wrong number. Carry on. Goodnight."

He hangs up before I can respond.

I roll my eyes, but something about his voice

lingers—warm, flustered, the sound of someone caught sneaking into the wrong classroom.

The second time, it's past midnight, and I'm at my kitchen counter inhaling leftover *siomai* and instant noodles, debating whether to eat or just go straight to bed.

My phone pings.

It's a text.

Last minute cancellation again.

30 more burpees next session.

I blink at the message. What the actual hell.

I type furiously in response.

Sorry.

Who is this?

The answer comes almost immediately.

Not Paolo?

I stick my tongue out at the screen.

Still not Paolo.

The response pings like lightning.

Then who's suffering my training threats?

I smirk despite myself.

Edna.

A very tired PA with zero intention of doing burpees.

Sorry not sorry.

There's a beat, then another ping.

Hi Edna! I'm Zeke!

Future doctor, part-time gym torturer.

Promise I'm not a stalker.

Just really bad at saving contacts.

Against my better judgment, I laugh. Out loud. At past midnight, alone in my apartment.

It becomes a pattern.

Accidental texts. Wrong calls that somehow don't feel wrong.

One night, he sends me a blurry picture of his anatomy notes, ranting about a professor who thinks students don't need sleep.

"PA life agrees," I reply. *"Sleep is a myth. Caffeine is a food group."*

"At least you sit. I'm on my feet 12 hours a day, teaching people who think planking for 15 seconds equals death."

"That IS death," I shoot back.

Another night, I complain about my boss adding three new meetings to my schedule after eight in the evening.

"That should be illegal," he replies. *"Tomorrow, skip work. Come train with me. Or just hang out."*

"No thanks. My idea of cardio is chasing the president with papers to sign. Knowing you, hanging out will literally mean hanging from something."

"You're killing me, Short Stuff."

"How do you know I'm short?"

"Because you text like someone who glares up at skyscrapers in Megaworld, just because."

I laugh so hard I nearly choke on stale crackers.

The calls start next. Not accidents this time.

"Can't sleep," he says once, his voice a little husky with exhaustion. *"Thought maybe you couldn't either."*

He's right. I'm at the office again, staring at my boss' overflowing inbox.

"You're crazy," I mutter.

But I don't hang up. Because we both are.

Instead, we talk. About nothing. About everything.

He tells me he grew up with two brothers and endless sun, that his tan is permanent proof of being forced outdoors while everyone else gamed.

I tell him I was the bookish girl whose mother packed whitening lotion into every bag, though it never worked on the shadows under my eyes.

"You work too much," he says one night.

"You flirt too much," I retort.

"That wasn't flirting." His voice drops a notch. *"This is."*

I freeze. The silence crackles. My heart does a strange flip.

I hang up.

But the next night, I answer again.

By week four, I know his exam schedule, his favorite protein shake flavor, and his least favorite exercise (*"mountain climbers are Satan's work"*).

By week five, he knows how many sugars I sneak into

my coffee, the fact that I hum 90s pop songs when stressed, and that I keep three different planners because one is never enough.

"*Control freak,*" he teases.

"Muscle freak," I fire back.

He laughs so hard he coughs.

But sometimes it tilts serious.

"*You're always tired,*" he says during one call.

"So are you."

"*Yeah, but you're…different tired. You sound like you've forgotten how it feels not to be.*"

The words lodge in my throat. I change the subject.

Then for one week, there's only silence.

No late-night rants. No accidental pings.

I try not to notice.

I fail.

On Friday night, my phone finally buzzes.

Sorry.

Exams.

Didn't want to bother you.

My chest eases as I type my response.

You should have.

I'm excellent at distractions.

Both ways.

A minute later, the phone rings. His deep chuckle fills the line.

"*Okay, I'm all yours. Distract me please.*"

And I do.

For hours.

It happens on a Monday. Almost Tuesday.

I reach my apartment at nearly midnight after staying in the office until eleven.

My phone buzzes with his fourth call that evening. I haven't picked up the first three.

This time, I swipe to accept.

His voice crackles over the line without his usual opening jokes or jabs.

"Where are you? Are you okay?"

I stare at the screen. "What?"

"Are you okay?" he repeats.

I swallow hard. "Yeah. I was stuck at work finishing a presentation for my boss. He was asked to speak at a convention in Boracay at the last minute. He's traveling in the next few hours."

I hear him exhale slowly over the line. *"Oh. Good. You got me worried for a minute there. I must have drank three cans of Red Bull just so I could stay awake."*

"What?" I repeat. "Why?"

"You didn't answer," he says. *"Thought maybe something bad happened. I was one energy drink away from stalking your office."*

I stare at the phone again. It's the last thing I expect him to say, but it warms my empty stomach.

"Something did happen," I answer honestly. "Not bad. Not at all. But I was needed."

"Needed?"

"Yeah. There was something important to do—and I did it. That's got to mean something."

He's quiet for a few moments. Then he says, *"You know what I thought, the first time I heard your voice?"*

"What?"

"That you sounded tired. But underneath it, strong. You were carrying too much, but still carrying it anyway."

I blink away the sting in my eyes, throat tight. "That's… accurate."

"I like accurate," he says softly.

We don't talk for nearly half a minute, but I break the silence.

"Zeke? Still there?"

"Always here for you."

I don't know whether to laugh or cry at that.

"You wanna know what I'm carrying?"

"Hit me. I got all night. I didn't drink all those Red Bulls for nothing."

So I tell him.

About my father who had a real family aside from us. About my mother who lost the battle to two lumps in her ovaries shortly after I finished high school.

About my little brother who lives with my elderly grandparents in Bacolod City and goes to college at UNO-R. About my job that helps me carry them all.

And he listens.

We last nearly two months like this. Voices in the night, names and messages on screens.

Then one evening, he texts.

What if we stopped being just wrong numbers?

Coffee?

My stomach flips.

I should say no. I don't do things like this. My life is schedules, reminders, alarms.

Beyond those…I don't really know.

But my fingers type the answer from my heart before my brain can take over.

Sure.

He's waiting when I arrive at the all-hours coffee shop down the road from my building.

I recognize him immediately.

The sight of him is a little too much. Lean and tall, shoulders filling out a plain black T-shirt. His arms are ridiculous, roped with muscle, tan skin stretched over veins like a sketch out of a textbook.

His smile is immediate, almost blinding. It's the kind of smile that says he's been saving it for someone in particular.

"Edna?"

His voice is the same one that's lulled me through insomnia, the same laugh that's pulled me from exhaustion. Now it has a face, sharp-featured and sun-warmed, real enough to make me want to run or stay forever.

"Zeke," I breathe.

The moment feels strange and not strange at all.

He grins down at me. "You weren't kidding. Short Stuff."

Heat rushes to my cheeks. I'm just grateful that it's nighttime. "You weren't kidding. Gym Freak."

He buys me an iced latte. We sit. We talk. And it's too easy. His laugh is louder in person, his eyes darker, his presence somehow more magnetic than I'd prepared for.

I'm acutely aware of my chubby arms, my pale skin, the faint creases in my blouse. Next to him—tan, ripped, glowing with health—I feel like a before-photo from a makeover that never happened.

Halfway through, I excuse myself to the bathroom, stare into the mirror, and whisper, "Don't get carried away, Edna. This isn't for you."

When I come back, his smile falters. "You okay?"

"I just...I don't know what you're expecting," I say, words tumbling before I can stop them. "You're..." I gesture helplessly at his broad chest, his impossible shoulders. "And I'm..."

I take a deep breath. Then I say it.

"This could all just be what it really was."

He regards me curiously, one eyebrow slightly lifted. "And what's that?"

"A mistake."

His chair scrapes back. He's in front of me before I can retreat, towering, his presence like heat and shadow.

"Don't," he says softly. "Don't compare us like that. I didn't spend months falling asleep to your voice because of what you look like. I came here for you."

I blink up at him, stomach clenching with nerves. "But what if this screws it up?"

His jaw tightens. Then he crouches down in front of me and leans over, close enough that his breath brushes my cheek. "Then let me screw it up properly."

And he kisses me.

It's not a tentative brush. It's not even a polite or platonic peck.

It's a collision.

It's hot and urgent, months of exchanged emojis and midnight laughter pouring into one desperate press of lips.

He tastes like coffee and heat and something I don't want to let go of. His mouth moves against mine with a confidence that makes my knees buckle, his hand sliding to the small of my back to steady me, dragging me closer until I'm flush against him.

I gasp, and he swallows the sound, deepening the kiss until the world lurches. My hands clutch his shirt, fingers bunching fabric over muscle that feels like steel under my palms.

When he finally pulls back, both of us are breathing like we've run a marathon. His lips still hover at my jaw as he rasps, "Still think this is a mistake?"

I shake my head, dizzy and overwhelmed.

"Best wrong number of my life."

Two nights later, I stumble out of the office at almost ten in the evening, shoes pinching, tote heavy with paperwork for an upcoming board meeting.

My phone buzzes.

It's a message from Zeke.

Look up.

I frown, then obey.

And there he is.

He's perched on a low wall separating our building from the one next to it. He's still in his gym tee, arms crossed, watching me like I'm the only thing worth seeing.

Before I can scold him for waiting so late and not telling me he's there, he jumps down and strides over.

Then he scoops me up like I weigh nothing, lifting me clean off the ground.

"Zeke!" I squeak, kicking uselessly, my arms flying around his neck.

"Relax, Short Stuff," he murmurs against my ear. "I'll always be here to help you carry it all. Starting with you."

I bury my face in his shoulder, laughing breathlessly as he spins me once, the city blurring around us.

For the first time in forever, I don't feel tired.

I feel alive.

All because of a mistake that led me to where I'm meant to be.

CHAPTER 2

THE MORNING COMMUTE

THE BUS ALWAYS SMELLS FAINTLY OF COFFEE AND RAIN. Even when it hasn't rained. Even when I have already finished the coffee in my trusty steel flask.

And I don't know his name.

Not for months.

But I know his routine as well as my own.

He boards at the second stop after mine. He takes the same seat, third row from the back, by the window. He always rests his bag between his feet.

I've grown familiar with the way he tilts his head slightly when reading something on his phone. His eyes have a faint golden-brown glow whenever they catch the morning sun.

His hair is longish and impossibly thick. He has a habit of running a hand through it whenever the traffic barely budges in the bus lane.

And he smiles at me whenever he catches me staring.

Like an idiot, I always smile back. Depending on my day, I sometimes throw in a nod.

That's all we ever do.

The world outside is usually a blur of billboards, puddles, and students dragging heavy backpacks, but inside, time feels different whenever he's there.

My time on the bus somehow feels measured, contained in our own little world. As if we're all part of the same little ritual before the city swallows us whole.

Every morning we exist together like this. Parallel, smiling, but never touching.

It happens on a Tuesday.

The bus is unusually crowded. People stand shoulder to shoulder, muttering apologies, holding onto metal poles as the driver lurches us forward.

When I step in, my usual seat is gone. So is the backup seat, and the backup to the backup. The only spot left is next to him.

I hesitate, heart racing like I've been caught doing something illegal. But the driver honks, the aisle clogs, and my choices vanish. I slide into the seat, trying not to breathe too loudly.

He glances up from his phone, surprise flickering in his eyes.

But then he smiles. Not the polite kind, but the kind that belongs only to me.

"Hi," he says. His voice is lower than I expected. It's calm, almost soothing.

"Hi," I echo, clutching my oversized tote to my chest like a shield.

"It's gonna be a long ride today," he says, nodding toward the packed aisle.

"Yeah," I say. "Guess we'll have to survive it together."

His laugh is small but genuine. "Guess so."

It isn't much. Just a few syllables each, but it's enough to make the ride feel different. Enough to make me wish the traffic was worse.

After that morning, something changes.

We don't talk every day, not at first. But some mornings, when the bus feels less like a coffin and more like a coffee shop, we speak.

He tells me his name is Santi. He works at an architecture firm half a block away from his stop. He spends his days trapped in meetings and his nights sketching on napkins or receipt paper because "ideas never show up on schedule."

I tell him I'm Gina. I work at a publishing house, mostly behind the scenes, making sure commas behave and deadlines don't explode. I share a love-hate relationship with my red pen, but it's the very thing that has gotten me places.

We swap mundane fragments of our lives.

"My landlady feeds all the strays in our street," I tell him.

"Cats?" he asks.

"Dogs. Six of them. They bark like a choir every morning."

He grins. "Better than an alarm clock."

"Why architecture?" I ask one morning.

"Because buildings don't move," he says. Then, in a softer voice, he adds, "Unlike people."

He asks about the books I carry sometimes. I ask about the playlist that leaks faintly from his headphones when he forgets to lower the volume.

Our conversations are stitched together from the small, the ordinary, the kind of details you don't tell strangers.

Because we're not strangers anymore.

Then, one Monday, he doesn't get on.

Tuesday, the seat is empty again.

Wednesday, still no Santi.

I tell myself it's silly to notice. People change routines. People oversleep. People have real lives outside my narrow hour of the morning.

But his absence feels…wrong. My stop feels heavier. The ride feels endless.

By Thursday, I stop looking at the window. I keep a book open but never read a line. I bite my lip until it hurts.

On Friday, I step onto the bus, preparing myself for another empty space.

And then he's there.

Third row from the back, hair messier than usual, tie knotted badly, eyes shadowed. Relief floods me so strongly I almost laugh out loud.

I sit beside him before I can stop myself.

"You disappeared," I say, a little too quickly and accusingly.

He looks guilty. "Work trip. Last minute. I should have said something."

"You don't owe me that," I say quickly, but I know my voice betrays me.

He studies me for a second.

After a while, he says softly, "You noticed."

"Of course I noticed," I admit, heat rushing to my cheeks. "You're…" I falter as my brain searches frantically for an explanation. "You're part of my mornings."

He smiles. "You're part of mine, too, Gina."

And that's the first time I realize I've been holding my breath all week.

The next Friday, the sky falls apart.

Rain pours so heavily it feels like the bus is sailing instead of driving. Everyone boards drenched, umbrellas dripping, shoes squeaking.

At his stop, Santi slides in beside me, shirt damp at the shoulders. A drop of rain clings stubbornly to his hair.

Without thinking, I reach into my tote and pull out a tissue. "Here."

He takes it, brushing the water away. "Thanks."

"You're dripping on my sleeve," I say lightly.

"You're complaining," he says right back, "but you haven't moved away."

"Maybe I don't mind."

Despite the weather, he gives me a broad, sunny grin.

The bus rattles over a puddle, throwing us against each

other for a moment, shoulder to shoulder, knee to knee. My pulse forgets how to count.

The storm roars outside, but inside, it's strangely quiet.

"I'd miss you," I say suddenly, my throat almost catching at the suddenness of the admission.

He turns to look at me closely. "What?"

"If you weren't here," I murmur, a blush rising from my collar. "If you stopped taking this bus. I'd miss you."

There's a long pause. His eyes light up, then shimmer.

I don't know what he's thinking. All I know is that he doesn't stop staring at me.

"I'd miss you, too," he says softly. "I'd really miss you."

The windows blur. The bus keeps moving.

But I feel something change.

Something seems to snap into place, unable to let go.

Weeks later, he finally says it, one drizzling morning.

As the bus nears my stop, he fidgets too noticeably, then finally says, "Dinner?"

His voice is steady, but his eyes aren't. They flick from my face to a spot above my shoulder.

"Dinner?" I echo.

"Off the bus," he clarifies, smiling nervously. "Some place real. I think we're overdue."

My heart kicks against my ribs.

"Yes," I say. "Definitely."

The bus rattles to a halt at my stop.

Passengers push into the aisle, umbrellas colliding, voices spilling out into the drizzle.

Santi steps down first, then turns back with his hand held out, waiting for me. When I take it and join him on the slick pavement, he leans closer. The rain threads between us, soft and silver.

For a moment, the whole gray, wet city feels hushed.

And then he kisses me.

It tastes like rain and coffee. It carries the weight and memory of every morning that brought us to this moment.

When he pulls back, he reaches for my cheek, brushing a damp, errant strand of my hair away.

"I'm glad you sat beside me that day," he says quietly.

"So am I," I answer.

Behind us, the bus pulls away, obedient to its route. But we walk in the other direction, away from the stop, toward something that feels a lot like home.

Months from now, maybe years, I'll still think of the first morning we spoke.

Of umbrellas dripping ghosts and memories onto the floor. Of tissues brushing away the rain.

Of glances and smiles louder than the traffic.

The bus still smells like coffee and rain.

But now, it smells like a story.

A story from something as everyday as the routine of two people making their way through a rain-drenched city.

A story of love that began with a morning commute.

CHAPTER 3

THE TRAIN THAT DIDN'T STOP

I MEET HIM ON THE WORST DAY OF MY LIFE.

The air is sticky with summer heat, the kind that clings to my skin and makes everything feel heavier than it is. I have just quit my job at the BPO. My apartment lease has ended. My father, who has already forgotten my name, has finally forgotten my face.

And the train is late.

I sit on the steel bench of the platform with my suitcase between my feet and a knot behind my ribs, wondering if it's too dramatic to just cry in public.

He sits two benches down, headphones in, tapping a pencil against a worn, leather-bound notebook.

I don't notice him at first. He is too quiet, too still—a shadow that has forgotten it isn't supposed to be noticed. But then he looks up, and our eyes meet, and something inside me trips.

He smiles like I'm a secret he already knows.

I look away.

Ten minutes later, he walks over and offers me a slightly squished sandwich in a plastic container.

"I'm not hungry," I say, even though I haven't eaten since yesterday evening.

He shrugs and places it beside me anyway, then takes a seat.

"The food in the station sucks. I got this sandwich from a vendor I've known since I was five. So this one's not poisoned. Probably."

I don't remember why I laugh, only that I do. And it's the first time something doesn't hurt in days.

His name is Leon.

He is a sketch artist. He draws strangers on trains and leaves the portraits behind—between pages of abandoned books, folded inside vending machine slots, under empty coffee cups. He says he likes the idea of someone finding a version of themselves they don't know exists.

"Why do you leave them?" I ask.

"Because art shouldn't beg to be kept."

He never asks where I'm going.

I never ask where he's from.

There's a kind of reverence in our silence, the way two people can exist next to each other without taking apart the ache they carry. He doesn't pry into my sorrow. I don't poke at his shadows. We just…sit there.

When the train finally comes, we board together.

He helps me hoist my suitcase into the overhead rack, then settles across from me. Not beside, but across. As if even now, he knows distance is safer.

He draws for two hours straight while I stare out the window pretending not to look at him.

When I finally doze off, he places a folded piece of paper in my lap.

It is me.

But not the broken, hollow me I see in mirrors. This girl is still bent, yes, but blooming anyway. Wind in her hair, scratches on her arms, fire in her eyes.

When I wake, he is gone.

It takes almost a year before I see him again.

He is standing in a bookstore, at a mall near the station, holding a cup of coffee and arguing with a child about whether unicorns can fly.

(They can't, he posits. They don't even exist. The child insists they do, and they most definitely *can*.)

I stand there too long, holding a book I'm not reading, watching him laugh like nothing has changed.

He looks up.

And again, he smiles like he already knows me.

"You forgot your sandwich," he says, as if a year hasn't happened.

"You ran off the train."

"You snored."

"I did not."

"You did."

He buys me the same drink as his. We sit on the coffee shop's wooden stools and watch people rushing around us.

The mall's crowded, but I feel still. Almost at peace.

He doesn't ask where I've been. I don't ask why he disappeared.

But when I reach into my bag that night, I find a sketch folded between my umbrella and tiny portable fan.

This time, it's both of us. On a train that never arrives. Sitting across from each other. Still not touching.

He texts me. We meet again. And again.

At the same coffee shop near the bookstore.

We become something close to almost.

Not quite friends. Not quite lovers. Always somewhere between.

He calls when the sky is the color of regret. I answer when my bones feel too hollow.

We walk, or sit, or breathe together in alleys and parks and bookstores way past closing time.

We haunt tables in the shadows of all-hours convenience stores, eating cup noodles like a ritual. Chicken for him, beef for me.

He drops me off at my boardinghouse on his rent-to-own motorcycle.

Once, I ask if he believes in fate.

He says, "Only when it's too late."

I fall in love with him in moments.

When he saves a moth from a coffee shop window and tells it, gently, "Not today."

When he cries watching a rerun of a movie where a pack of sled dogs gets left behind.

When he touches my wrist like he's afraid of breaking the air between us.

But Leon is like fog.

He arrives when I'm not looking and leaves before I can hold on.

One time, he tells me, softly, "Some people are just stopovers, not destinations."

I nod as if I agree. Or at least understand.

But I'm already building a home at the station of my heart.

The night he tells me goodbye, it doesn't rain.

It should, I think.

We sit at the same platform where we first met, now strangers all over again.

"I got accepted," he says.

"To what?"

"A Fine Arts scholarship. You know, at the university. In the city."

My throat closes around the word *stay*, so I smile instead.

"Wow, that's awesome. Congratulations."

He reaches into his bag and hands me a notebook. The same old leather one he always carries.

I undo the silver magnetic button.

Inside are sketches.

Me, again and again.

Me laughing. Me angry. Me walking away. Me staring out a train window, always alone.

"I don't know why it's always you, Jen," he tells me quietly.

"I do," I answer, just as softly.

He smiles his knowing smile, one last time.

"Of course you do."

He kisses my forehead, stands, and walks onto the train.

I don't follow.

He doesn't look back.

I still take the train sometimes.

I sit on the platform and wait for a shadow to sit two benches down and offer me a sandwich.

It never happens.

But sometimes, when the sky is the color of regret and the wind tastes like a name you haven't said in years, I pull out his sketches and hold them close to my chest.

I still don't know if Leon is real.

Maybe he is a dream dressed in skin.

Maybe he is just another train I never board.

But I hope—god, I hope—somewhere in the big city, there's a drawing of me.

Smiling. Standing. Finally whole.
Maybe, in that version, I get on the train.
Maybe, in that version, he stays.
Maybe.
Always maybe.

CHAPTER 4

THE LIGHT IN THE WINDOW

I DON'T KNOW WHO HE IS.

I don't even know what he does for a living.

Not for the first three months, anyway.

But I know that he makes coffee at exactly 6:04 every morning. I know that he reads by the window with his feet curled under him like a cat. I know that he waters his plants every three days, even if it rains. I know that he leaves his window open during thunderstorms, but unrolls a makeshift tarp to keep the wind and water out.

And I know that his lamp glows until almost midnight, flicking off a few seconds before mine.

I don't mean to watch. Not at first. I only notice because his apartment is across from mine—diagonal, close enough to see into when the curtains are open, far enough that the details blur.

He's quiet, almost gentle, by nature. He doesn't play

loud music or have people over. He moves like he doesn't want to bother the floor.

In a city that's crowded, loud, and constantly moving, his quiet is magnetic.

I call him Window Boy in my head.

Window Boy with his thick black hair almost always tousled, with his slightly lopsided silver-rimmed glasses.

I know how he looks the same way I know my favorite digital print.

The first time we acknowledge each other, it's barely more than a glance. Or maybe a blink exchange.

I'm standing by my kitchen counter with a bowl of noodles. It's almost midnight. I look up, and he's at his window, watching the rain.

He sees me.

I see him.

We freeze at the same time.

A heartbeat of stillness.

Then, shyly, he lifts his hand. He gives me a small, tentative wave.

I wave back.

He smiles. Just a little.

Just enough.

That night, I sleep better than I have in weeks.

We fall into a rhythm.

We wave in the mornings now. I sip my awful green tea, he sips coffee.

Sometimes I hold up a book, and he nods like he approves.

Once, he held up a notebook with a post-it stuck to it that said, *"What are you reading today?"*

I wrote my answer on printer paper and held it up. *"Never Let Me Go, Kazuo Ishiguro."*

He made a little heart with his hands.

I decide he's a little bit of a nerd, just like me.

It was stupid. And sweet.

It made my whole day quieter in the best way.

If this is peace, then I want it.

I learn his habits. He likes chicken-flavored instant noodles with egg. He folds laundry with perfect corners, always starting with the largest pieces. He takes his time drinking his coffee, inhaling and sipping in turn, causing his glasses to fog up.

He learns mine too. He knows when I'm working late. He knows when I'm too tired to cook and eat crackers at the window instead. He knows when I'm sad, even if I'm smiling.

I can tell because he sends a small, thoughtful gesture across the distance. Sometimes it's a thumbs up or a peace sign; other times it's a paper swan or a slightly wilted flower stuck to the glass.

I keep a journal now, a weird little A4 document online that I update every day before bed. The template is a rich pink, bordered with white hearts and fluffy cats.

Day 42: He wore blue again. The good blue. The soft one.

Day 55: We both held up ramen at the same time. It felt like a conversation.

Day 61: He waved goodnight. I waved back late. He waited. He didn't even move from his spot.

I don't write about work. Or my family. Or my loneliness. I only write about him.

One night, the storm hits hard.

The kind that knocks power out in entire blocks with one strong gust.

My apartment goes dark. I scramble for candles. For a moment, the city feels swallowed.

I move to the window out of habit.

His apartment is dark too.

But then, a flashlight flicks on.

He's there, holding it up. It casts a soft beam in the shape of a smile.

I lift my candle.

He sits by the window with it, just holding the light between us.

We stay like that for almost an hour, two shadows in the dark, watching the storm unravel.

I press my hand to the glass.

After a moment, he does the same.

Our palms don't touch, not really. But I feel something pass through the pane.

A stillness. A warmth.

A maybe.

The first note appears two days later.

In plain white paper, folded and taped to my door. The handwriting inside is neat, slender, and no-nonsense.

"Hi. I'm Winston. I'm sorry if it's weird, but I asked the

security guard which unit had the girl who always reads in the window. I'd like to know your name. If that's okay."

"PS: You have excellent taste in instant noodles."

I laugh so loudly I scare my neighbor's cat. It gives me a judgmental stare before padding off down the corridor.

I write back.

"Hi Winston. I'm Charlene. And yes, it's okay. I've been calling you Window Boy in my head, so this is a huge upgrade."

"PPS: I have excellent taste in many things."

The next day, a new note appears.

"I'm sure you do. Want to prove it? Coffee?"

Our first real, face-to-face conversation doesn't happen until three weeks later.

We meet at the corner café a block away.

He's taller in person. Warm and good-natured, but nervous in a way that makes me feel braver.

His good blue shirt is slightly untucked from his jeans in one corner.

I decide, right then and there, that I like him.

We talk for three hours. About everything. About nothing. It's easy.

He listens like I'm a song he's trying to learn by heart.

When we say goodbye, he doesn't kiss me.

He just gives my hand a quick squeeze and says, "I'll see you at the window."

And I do.

Every day. Every night.

It's like clockwork. A comfort I almost crave like air, something I didn't know I needed until it was right there through the glass.

We fall in love through the window.

With scribbled signs. With matching cups. With watching the same movie and reacting in real time, holding up rating cards we made for each other. Mine has his choice of old laptop cardboard boxes cut into squares; his are colored pink and decorated with fluffy cats in varying moods.

We meet on weekends. We get takeout and hang out at his place.

We take long walks in the neighborhood. Somehow, it always happens right after there's rain, when it feels like something's coming back to life.

In late-night conversations, he tells me things slowly, almost thoughtfully. I learn not to rush the quiet.

He kisses me in the elevator once, just before the doors open for him to step out. I giggle for three floors afterward. My neighbor's cat judges me once more, but I can see the grudging approval now.

One time, after sharing a bucket of fried chicken for dinner, he brushes a strand of hair behind my ear like it's the most natural thing in the world.

It is.

The day we say *I love you*, it happens at the window.

No theatrics. No music.

Just two people holding up signs at the same time, accidentally, ridiculously in sync.

On white cardboard, his says: *"I think I'm falling for you."*

On a pink A4 with fluffy cats, mine answers: *"I already love you."*

We both start laughing. Then crying. Then laughing again.

Later, he comes over and kisses me like my laughter is a secret he finally knows.

And I think maybe we always knew this was going to happen.

From the very first wave. From the first silence we filled together.

Now, I watch him sleep on my couch. He fell asleep halfway through a movie. His coffee's gone cold on the table. His glasses slide down his nose.

I take a blanket from the closet and tuck it around his long limbs. I take his glasses off and put it carefully on the table.

I kiss him on the lips, then rise slowly.

Even though he's here with me, I press my hand to the window.

Out of habit. Out of gratitude.

I can see it's drizzling.

The apartment across from mine is dark now. It looks still, but not empty. Not really.

It's filled with the silence between two heartbeats.

It's full of memory. Of promise. Of waiting.

Of my love for my Window Boy.

And this time, when I reach for the glass, I feel him put his palm over my knuckles.

His other arm goes around my waist. He presses his lips to my hair.

"Hi," he murmurs.

"Hi," I echo.

He feels warm.

Real. Close enough to hold.

At last.

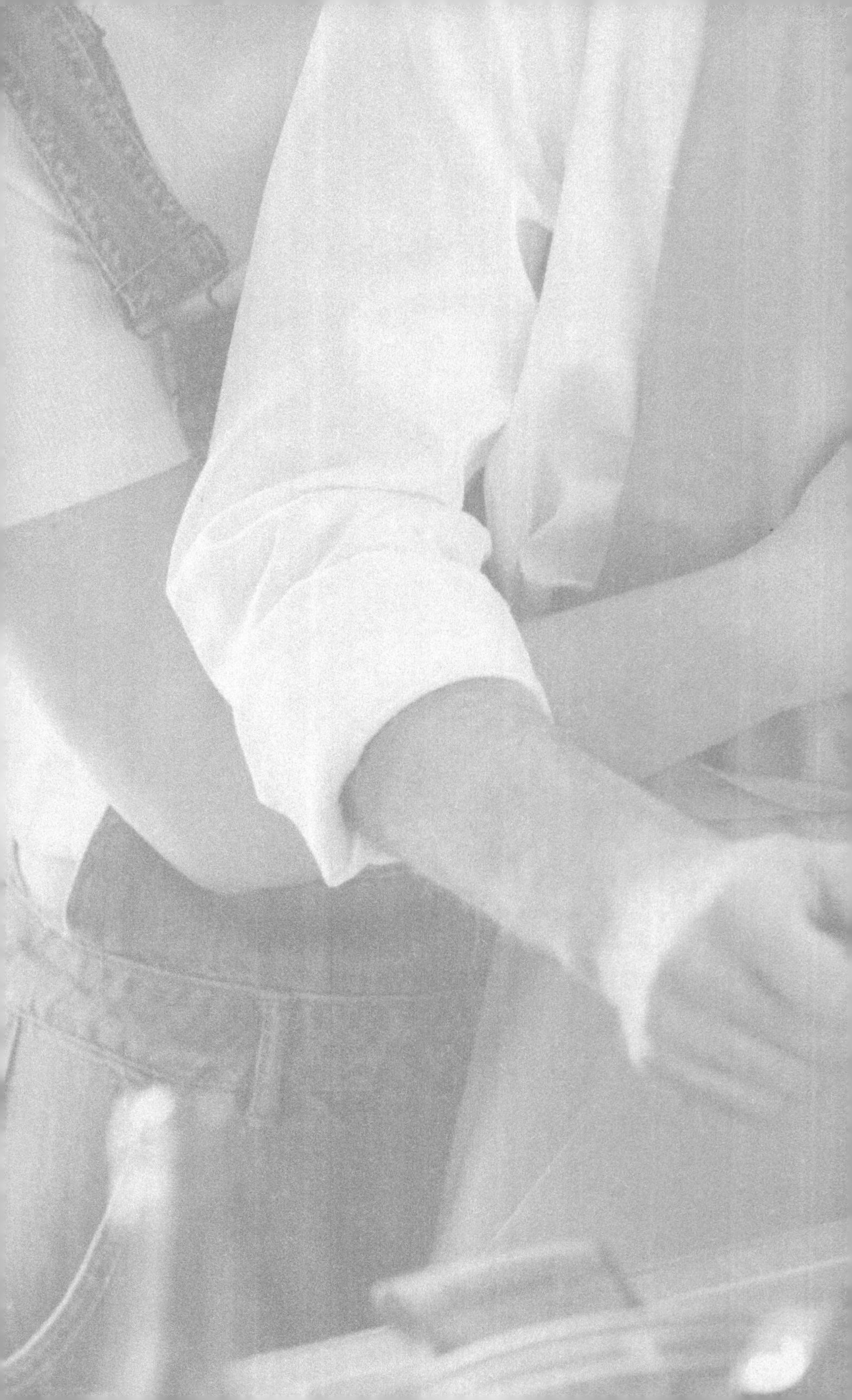

CHAPTER 5

THE TASTE OF HER SMILE

I DON'T THINK SHE KNOWS I EXIST.

But I wait for her.

The kitchen is hot and loud, full of shouting, sizzling, and grease spattering. I stay in the back, quietly, cleaning pots or restocking the line.

I don't have a real chef title, just a name tag and the apron. Just a dream I keep pressed under my tongue.

She walks by the side entrance at exactly 8:47 every week, heels clicking on the concrete, hair tied up in a way that makes her neck look fragile. Her dress always looks expensive. Her smile never quite reaches her eyes.

I watch her through the screen door. The others don't notice her. Or maybe they do, but not the way I see her.

I leave a small container out by the alley gate every Friday night. Always something different. Bone broth when it rains. A *bao* bun with pork and ginger when the wind stings. Fresh mango slices when the air gets heavy and humid. Nothing fancy. Nothing that would be missed.

Sometimes, when I peek after my shift, the container is empty.

Sometimes, she's sitting on the curb with it in her hands, legs tucked under her, heels abandoned beside her.

I don't say anything. I just watch her eat like she hasn't eaten all day.

Once, she left a flower.

A tiny carnation, half-wilted, tucked into the empty bowl.

The following Friday, I added fried rice.

She's not like the others who come to the restaurant—the socialites, the fashion influencers, the girls who take pictures with their food and barely touch it.

She shows up in pageants and fashion shows, sometimes. I see the posters outside the mall. Her name is Mara. She always looks flawless. Perfect cheekbones, large eyes. Painted lips and a graceful posture.

But up close, when she doesn't know I'm looking, she moves like she's about to fall apart.

One Friday, she doesn't show up.

I wait until ten. The food grows cold. My chest feels like it's been scraped out.

The next week, she returns.

She looks paler and thinner. Her collarbones are sharper than I remember. Her lipstick is smudged. She walks slower, hobbling a little on her high heels. That night, I make congee with chicken and egg.

I put it by the alley door.

When I come back for cleanup, she's there.

But this time, she looks up.

"It was you," she says.

Her voice is soft, hollow. She sounds exhausted.

I freeze at the sound, eyes taking in the state of me. My apron is caked with work. My hands are stained with paprika and smell like garlic.

She smiles. Not the smile on her posters, but a real one. The one that looks like it might break.

"Thank you."

I nod.

"I didn't know how to eat anymore," she says quietly. "But you reminded me."

I nod again, and I flee.

After that night, she comes to the restaurant.

Not through the front, never with the other guests. Always the back, through the kitchen. Always the quiet seat near the door, where she can smile at me. My boss lets her in without question.

She doesn't order. She just waits.

And I bring her food.

Chicken *adobo*. *Tortang talong*. Fresh tomatoes and scrambled eggs over garlic rice. Meals I make in between orders. Meals from home. Meals I remember my mother cooking when I had no appetite.

I ask my boss to deduct the cost from my wages, but Miss Salma says it's okay. She's a fan; maybe Mara will get a title in the next Miss Philippines. She crosses her fingers and grins at me conspiratorially.

Mara always finishes whatever I make for her. She starts to kiss me goodnight, on the cheek. She hugs Miss Salma and thanks her, promising to do her best in the competitions.

And every time she leaves the restaurant through the kitchen door, she looks a little brighter.

One night, I catch her humming as she sits on a step outside the kitchen. The restaurant has a private party inside, but she still chooses to stay.

It's the kind of sound that fills a room, even when it's small. She sounds like she's trying to keep the darkness away.

She hums until her lips start to tremble. Then she stops.

"It's getting harder, Bobby," she tells me. "They want me to be smaller. Thinner. Lighter. I tried. But it hurts now. Everything hurts."

I bring her chicken corn soup. I put it on a stool next to her, so she can reach the bowl easily.

She eats it slowly. Every spoonful to her mouth feels like a prayer.

I don't know how to say the things I want to say. That she doesn't have to disappear to be loved. That food is not the enemy. That she could stay here forever, and I would feed her until the world forgets how to be cruel.

Instead, I say, "I put extra ginger. For your throat. You know, for the question-and-answer portion."

She smiles.

"You always know."

One night, she walks up to me.

It's after close. The kitchen is dim, only the emergency light glowing by the fridge. I'm peeling *kamote* for the sugared fritters she likes, and she's sitting cross-legged on the counter.

Then she steps down quietly. Her head finds my shoulder like it belongs there.

"Don't stop," she says. "Cooking, I mean. Even if I'm not here."

My hands freeze midway.

"You'll always be here," I say, as bravely as I can, smiling through the ripping ache in my chest. "Right?"

She doesn't answer.

Instead she leans in and kisses me.

I kiss her back.

The *kamote* is forgotten.

She takes me up to her apartment, where we make love on her pink-and-white sheets with the red ladybugs.

I don't sleep, but she does. I hold her, and I watch her.

In the morning, I make her breakfast of eggs and toast. I prepare to leave when she gets a reminder that her call time is at ten.

But as she kisses me goodbye, she tells me, "I love you, Bobby."

I put my arms around her and I say it right back.

I leave with the taste of breakfast and her in my heart.

The next Friday, she doesn't come back to the building.

Or the next.

Or the one after.

I wait. I cook. I leave her the *kamote* fritters by the door.

But the container stays full.

I find out from Miss Salma. She calls me into her tiny office, but I know the news before she even says it.

"Mara passed away yesterday," she chokes. "Complications from malnutrition, I think. They said she hid it well. They told me she fought while in the hospital, but her body was too weak."

I don't know what happened next, but I swear the world turned black.

And I heard screaming.

That night, I cook one last meal.

Chicken *adobo*—her absolute favorite. Rice shaped into a heart.

Chicken corn soup and cherry tomatoes for starters. *Kamote* fritters for dessert.

I sit on the step outside the kitchen, the way she used to. I eat in silence. Every bite tastes like goodbye.

When I finish, I close my eyes.

And for just a moment, I feel the weight of her head on my shoulder.

I hear her telling me to not stop cooking.

Like she never left.

Somewhere out there, I think she's smiling.

Somewhere, she's full. Warm and whole.

I keep cooking.

Because someone, somewhere, still needs to eat.

And because love, when it is true, always finds its way to the table.

CHAPTER 6

BOOKSHOP HOURS

IT STARTS AT THE POETRY SECTION.

He's always there before me, standing with his head slightly inclined, wavy black hair unruly, glasses sliding down his nose. He's always wearing a light-colored shirt over dark jeans and impeccably polished brown boots.

Sometimes he's flipping through Neruda, other times it's a thin chapbook I've never heard of. Other times he's at the non-fiction shelves frowning at autobiographies.

I pretend not to notice. I drift aimlessly, fingers grazing spines, heart hammering like I'm sixteen again.

I always end up picking something by Khalil Gibran. Other times I just go to women's fiction and pick Judith Krantz because I don't have the energy to get overly emotional.

Sometimes he steps aside to let me pass. Sometimes I do the same for him. We never say a word.

It's easier that way.

The shop itself is strange. It's a 24-hour secondhand bookstore and café in the middle of a city that never sleeps. It smells like old paper, burnt espresso, and rain from the sidewalk. The kind of place that feels like it doesn't belong in this timeline.

I come here because I don't know where else to go after work. My job drains me, my apartment feels empty, and here at least, there are books and people who don't ask questions.

And him.

Always him.

It becomes a pattern.

I see him tucked into the corner table with his laptop when he's not browsing.

And he sees me. I know he does.

Sometimes he leaves a scrap of paper on his table with a short verse written on the back.

I find the first one particularly gray and damp Thursday afternoon.

"Every day you play with the light of the universe."

For some reason, it makes me smile.

Three days later, I see another. This time, the words are from Gibran.

"Your pain is the breaking of the shell that encloses your understanding."

When I reach my apartment that night, I sit on the couch for an hour, crying at first, then laughing.

Then I cry again until my tears are all gone.

It's insane, but it's also the most alive I've felt in months.

The night it happens, the storm rolls in sudden and loud.

Thunder rattles the windows. Rain slams against the roof.

And then darkness.

The power cuts out, plunging the shop into shadow.

Gasps ripple from the handful of customers still inside. The barista and cashier fumble for emergency lamps and candles, muttering apologies.

I freeze near the poetry shelf, still clutching a worn copy of D.H. Lawrence's *Birds, Beasts and Flowers*, my phone torch shaky in my hand.

And then he's there.

"Hey," he says softly, his voice warmer than I imagined. "You okay?"

I nod, a little too fast. "Yeah. Just…wasn't expecting that."

He smiles, the kind that glows even in the dim light. "Guess we're stuck until the storm passes. Or at least until the power comes back on."

I nod again, my pulse kicking hard.

His smile grows wider. "Unless you wanna brave the rain and the wind—and the dark? In which case, chivalry dictates I should escort you to safety."

A smile blooms across my face, no matter how hard I try to play it cool.

"You sound like you belong in the wrong century," I say.

He shakes his head. "Chivalry is never out of century or style." He extends a hand. "Well? Into the storm? Through the dark?"

I giggle, shaking my own head in response.

"No," I answer, taking his hand. "To the corner table."

He leads me to his usual table, and pulls out a chair for me.

After I take my seat, he disappears into the shadows of the darkened shop and returns minutes later with two glasses of iced chocolate topped with cream and real chocolate shavings.

"Someone ran off before they got their order," he says simply, as he puts the first glass before me. "Didn't want these two perfectly untouched servings of iced choco to go to waste."

"Very smart," I intone. "How much do I owe you?"

He takes the seat across from mine. "Nothing. It's on the house."

I eye him closely. "Or on you?"

He tilts his head with a broad grin, his teeth gleaming white in the dim light. "You could say both."

That explains a lot. The constant presence. The way he moves around the shop with such quiet, comfortable familiarity.

"Well, thanks," I say, feeling a little warm at the way his eyes can't seem to look away from me, now that we're seated face to face.

"I've seen you here before," he says, taking a sip of his drink.

I laugh nervously. "Yeah. I've…seen you too."

"Poetry shelf, right?" His eyes crinkle. "You almost always reach for the same side. Gibran fan. Sometimes D.H. Lawrence."

I flush. "And you always pretend not to notice."

"Guilty." He leans in. "I'm Carlo."

"Alice." My name feels fragile, new as I say it to someone else.

He grins. "It suits you."

We talk through the storm, through the dark.

About books, about music, about why I haunt this place like a restless ghost. I admit I come here because I don't know where else to go when I can't stand my own walls, after a long dreary day of evaluating health insurance claims.

He tells me he used to work abroad, teaching technical English in the vast oil fields of Saudi Arabia. But something about the written word brought him home and made him start his own printing press, all digital, able to cater to more modest runs from smaller publishers. He'd bought this bookstore from a National Artist of Literature as a passion project a few years ago, then added an all-hours coffee shop as a nod to their family business in Iloilo.

Somehow it's easy. Too easy. It's as if we've been in a conversation for months without saying a word until now.

The candles flicker. The storm softens. But his eyes never leave mine.

When the power finally comes back on, most people clap in relief. But I feel disappointment sink in my chest.

"Looks like we're free," I murmur.

"Yeah." He hesitates, then says, "Or…we could stay a little longer."

Something in his voice makes my breath catch.

I nod. "Yeah. Let's."

He takes my hand and we drift back to the poetry shelf, side by side this time. He pulls out a thin volume, flips to a page, and hands it to me.

Read this, his eyes seem to say.

I read aloud, my voice trembling a little, but steady enough to form the words.

"I want to do with you what spring does with the cherry trees."

Silence.

His hand brushes mine tentatively, asking.

I don't pull away.

Then he leans closer, carefully, giving me time to change my mind.

I don't.

The kiss is soft at first, a promise more than a question. But when I tilt my head up toward his and press my lips back harder, it deepens.

It becomes warm and insistent, then hot and dizzying. His hand cradles my jaw, the other finds its way to my waist. My arms reach up, anchoring myself to his shoulders.

I forget the storm. I forget the silence of my apartment, the ache of empty nights. I forget the grayness of days and tasks that never really end.

There's only the taste of him, the heat of him, the impossible, undeniable rightness of this moment.

When we break apart, both of us are breathing hard. He puts his arms around me and draws me close.

"I've been waiting," he admits, voice raw. "Alice in my bookshop."

I giggle, then gasp as he kisses me again.

"Me, too," I murmur. "Me too."

We leave together just before dawn.

The streets glisten from the storm, puddles glowing under streetlamps. The air smells of wet asphalt and earth, the city quieter than I've ever known it.

Carlo drives me to my block in a neat black sedan, then insists on escorting me to my apartment. We walk close enough that our arms brush now and then. Neither of us rushes.

At my door on the second floor, he hesitates.

"So…" His voice is careful, almost shy. "This is you?"

I nod. "Yeah. End of the line. Consider your knightly duties fulfilled, sir."

He smiles, but it wavers.

And I understand why.

He doesn't want the night to end either.

Something inside me clicks with certainty, gentle and tender.

I look at him, really look, at his hair damp from rain, the warmth in his eyes that I've been waiting months to touch, the gentle hands that have written and shared poetry with me.

"You could come in," I say softly. "If you want."

His breath catches.

A pause, then he nods, a slow smile lighting up his face. "Yeah. I want."

My hands shake a little unlocking the door, but when it swings open, the world feels warmer and steadier.

And when I step into my four walls, it somehow feels new this time.

He steps inside with me.

I close the door behind him.

And whatever happens after belongs only to us.

The sunlight through my curtains feels different.

Softer. Less lonely.

Carlo is still here, clad only in shorts and barefoot in my kitchen, chucking quietly as he gets my old coffee machine to work.

"Coffee is in your genes," I say softly.

He glances up when he catches me watching him from the narrow doorway. "Hey."

"Hey." My voice is rough with sleep, but my smile feels easy.

He crosses the room and takes me into his arms without

hesitation, pressing a warm, wet kiss to my mouth. I squeal when his tongue sneaks in.

I punch him lightly on the chest when he draws back to pull out a chair at the tiny kitchen table. As soon as I'm seated, he puts a steaming mug of coffee in front of me, followed by a plate of perfectly made twin sunny side-up.

"So…I'll see you tonight?"

I laugh, the sound bubbling out of me before I can stop it.

"Yeah," I say. "I'll see you at the shop."

He shakes his head as he takes the seat next to mine.

"No. I'm picking you up as soon as you finish work. We're going to look for new places to haunt together."

Then he leans over to kiss me again.

And I kiss him right back.

I don't even get to touch the eggs or the coffee, because I end up in his arms, laughing as he scoops me up and carries me back to bed.

And just like that, it isn't just about the bookshop or the walls around me anymore.

It's about everything after.

It's about everything beyond.

CHAPTER 7

SUN AND STEEL

THEY SAY I'M TOO LOUD, TOO SMART, TOO SOFT, TOO fat, too bright.

You can say I'm too much of everything.

And yet he barely speaks at all.

When I first meet him, he's the new gym instructor at the local wellness center where I work part-time.

He walks like he used to belong to something stricter, something stronger. He stands like he's waiting for orders that don't come anymore.

His arms are built like stone. He's always in black.

There's a scar across his left eyebrow. And a silence around him so thick it feels like history.

"You're not what I expected," I tell him after our third hallway pass.

He blinks. "What did you expect?"

"More...gym. Less assassin."

"Arys." He follows the name with the ghost of a smile. "Almost Marine."

That catches me. His face softens; his eyes crinkle at the corners, almost kindly.

I don't realize I stopped breathing for a second.

"Laurie," I answer, feeling a flush rise up my throat. "Almost lawyer."

He tells me later, when we're alone by the back stairwell during break time, that he didn't make it. He trained, enlisted, prepped. But then the migraines started. Then the blackouts. Then the diagnosis: a benign but inoperable growth near his brain stem. Not deadly. Not curable. Just...a permanent no.

"The body was willing," he says. "But the brain had other plans."

He says it like a joke. I hear the heartbreak in it.

I tell him about law school being put on indefinite pause.

"My dad passed away," I say. "A tumor in his throat. A year later, my mom followed. It was her breast this time. Life had other plans."

He nods solemnly. "I'm sorry."

I nod in thanks.

And when I do, he reaches for a lock of my hair, rolling it over his fingers.

Then he lets go.

I swallow hard and walk back into the center.

But his touch stays with me.

We become a strange kind of constant.

I start showing up early. I bring him coffee and fresh *puto* from the market.

We stay late, talking. I watch him train like he's still trying to earn a title he lost.

I start walking and stretching more. I ask him to show me routines.

It's not about weight at first. It's about strength. About being in my body and not apologizing for it.

But then he says, quietly, during a plank hold, "You're glowing lately."

Something inside me stirs. Just a little, but I feel it.

I start pushing harder.

He never asks me to. Never hints that he wants me to shrink. But I see how his eyes change when I walk into a room. How they linger longer.

And I want him to want me.

Not just as I am, but because I can be more.

More of the world he understands. Less of the softness that makes people underestimate me.

So I keep pushing.

We kiss for the first time after a staff party, when he drops me off at my boardinghouse.

I'm in a dress I never would have worn six months ago. It's form-hugging, nipped at the waist and bare at the arms. The dipped neckline teases what I've always been secretly proud of.

He looks at me like he's never seen me before.

"You clean up nice," he says.

"I was always nice."

"You were always beautiful," he replies.

I don't know what to do with that truth, so I lean in. My hand lands in the middle of his chest.

He leans down, all shadow and warmth.

The kiss is slow. It feels gentle. Honest.

It feels like a pact to break through each other's walls.

We make love one week later.

It happens in his tiny apartment. On his neatly-made bed.

The heat comes from his silence, his steely focus on what he could make me feel.

I tremble when I take my shirt off.

Not because I'm scared, but because this matters. Because this is the body I live in. The body I've fought with and fed and punished and tried to make smaller.

The body he touches like it is a gift.

He doesn't say anything when I cry. He just kisses my shoulders, and holds me so gently I almost fall apart.

And when we move together, it's feels as if we're made for this rhythm.

We sleep tangled, limbs soft and sore, our breath syncing in the dark.

I think it's the beginning of something.

It isn't.

He starts pulling away two months later.

Not cruelly. Just…less.

Shorter replies. Longer silences. Distance growing cobwebs in all the places we used to be close.

When I ask him if something's wrong, he shakes his head.

"Nothing's wrong. You're amazing. I'm just...tired."

I want to scream.

I want to ask if it's me. If I lost too much. If I lost what made me his.

If I'll never be enough, even if I lost it all.

But I don't.

But I think I already know.

I see it in the way he looks at the ocean when we pass it in his battered blue car. He looks like he's still out there, in a version of himself that didn't break. A version of him that wasn't told he couldn't be someone.

In a life where I was only a passing glance, a girl full and loud—not the girl who stayed.

We end things in the center's parking lot.

He doesn't cry. Neither do I.

He says, "You changed me."

I say, "You made me want to change."

He holds my face for a long time. "You'll find someone, Laurie. Someone better."

I laugh, because it's the last thing that's funny. "No one will be better. Just different."

He kisses my lips, then my forehead.

I reach up to caress the scar on his eyebrow.

"Goodbye, Arys."

And then he's gone.

A week later, he quits his job.

After a year, I meet someone else.

A science teacher at a private all-boys school, with messy hair and gentle hands who listens when I talk about starting law school again. He answers perfectly, and shares with me his plans to take his Doctorate in Education.

We start slow.

He likes to hold my hand. I let him.

When we kiss, I don't compare it.

But sometimes, in the quiet, I remember.

The push of muscle against mine.

The silence of a man who wanted to be steel and unbreakable and couldn't forgive himself for failing.

The first time I say *I love you* to the man I'm with now, he says it back without pause.

A week later, his sister, a friend who works out at the gym, tells me he's been looking at rings on layaway.

And still, I go to my room and cry in the shower.

Because love can be good and still not be first.

Because Arys taught me how to glow.

Because I still remember him.

The soldier who never was.

The man who kissed me like I was made of the sun.

The steely silence where I learned I could love without disappearing.

Even if it isn't him.

CHAPTER 8

TABLE FOR TWO

IT HAPPENS ON A DAY I WAS SUPPOSED TO BE celebrating.

It's a fucked-up kind of celebration, but still.

Instead, when I give my name to the hostess, she looks panicked.

"I'm so sorry, Mr. Alvarez, but we overbooked. The last available table…well, you'll have to share."

I frown. "Share?"

"Yes. If Miss Moran is willing to, of course." The hostess gestures to the woman in a red dress standing near the podium. I find myself looking into wide, intelligent eyes. She's medium height and shapely, with thick black hair that falls halfway down her back.

The woman stares at me, red lips pursed, clutching her phone like a lifeline.

Or a weapon.

Depends on the angle, really.

I can only blink at her in response. I try to open my mouth, but nothing comes out.

"It's fine," says the woman, not trying to disguise her annoyance. "It's not his fault, is it?"

"No, Miss Moran," says the hostess, lowering her eyes. "And I'm very sorry about this again. There must be something that happened to the booking system that day."

"Are there…other options?" I ask.

"Of course, sir." The hostess looks at the screen in front of her, and then back at me. "I'll have a table waiting for you in an hour and a half, if you're willing to wait."

"It's okay," I say, giving the woman in the red dress a tentative glance. I'm starving, so the possibility of a cellphone being swung at my head seems to be a risk worth taking. "If Miss Moran doesn't mind."

"I don't mind," she says, although the look she's giving me clearly says she does.

The manager comes over to the podium, apologizing profusely to the woman, and then to me. He recognizes me from previous visits and calls me a very valued regular guest. He promises that the meal will be waived and only the drinks will be charged.

"I'll take care of the drinks," I say, looking at the woman again.

She meets my eyes, holds my gaze for a few tense seconds, and finally nods.

"Fine."

So here we are.

Two strangers at a candlelit table, surrounded by couples leaning across glasses of wine to whisper secrets. The fact that we're in a five-star hotel makes it weirder than it already is.

Not exactly the Thursday night I had in mind.

For five minutes, we each act like the menus are suddenly the most fascinating works of literature on earth.

Finally, she sighs. "This is ridiculous."

I glance up. "The table-sharing thing or the fact that we're both pretending the other doesn't exist?"

Her lips twitch. "Both."

She closes her menu. "Look, I'll go first. I'm celebrating. In a way, at least. It's the one-year mark. My ex cleaned out my savings. Said he was investing. Turns out 'investing' meant bogus cryptocurrency schemes named after mythical beasts and a side girlfriend in Cebu. I came here to remind myself I can still buy my own damn dinner."

I choke on my water. "Wow. Hard act to follow."

Her eyebrows rise. "Your turn."

I rub the back of my neck. "Caught my fiancée cheating. On my birthday. With my cousin. In my apartment. Today's a year to the day I cleaned out all her stuff from my apartment."

She freezes mid-sip of her mocktail. "No."

"Yup. On the couch. Not really my idea of a surprise party, but there you go."

"Oh my God." She covers her mouth. "I'm so sorry. That's…horrible."

"It's fine." I shrug. "At least I got the cake."

That pulls a laugh out of her. A real one, soft and startled. "You didn't."

"I did. Chocolate mousse. Ate the whole thing while she tried to explain why my cousin was not wearing pants in my living room."

She shakes her head incredulously. "That's the stuff of afternoon TV dramas. Darkly impressive."

"I aim to please."

She lifts her glass in a mock toast. "Very gangsta. Really."

I lift my own glass of red wine. "To gangsta."

"To gangsta," she echoes.

"I'm Gene," I say as I put my glass down. I offer her the bread basket. "Gene Alvarez."

She takes a roll with sesame seeds, giving me a small smile. "Ashley Moran."

The food arrives then. Pasta for her, steak for me. Conversation trickles into something easier.

She tells me she works in finance. I tease her for not seeing through her ex's scam. She rolls her eyes and admits that sometimes a six-pack and perfect hair could be very distracting.

I tell her that I have my own business, third-party industrial laundry and cleaning services, that I inherited from my father, which I keep expanding all over the country. The hotel is one of my first clients when I joined the business at eighteen.

But then I tell her about the tragedy of last year's birthday, including the part where my cousin got into the rideshare wearing only his briefs, to the evil glee of my nosy neighbors in the apartment building.

She shares that her ex started seeing the side piece in Cebu because he felt she "validated" his chosen career as a lifestyle influencer, which meant a lot of abdominal close-ups on his social media reels.

By the time we finish the main course, she's laughing so hard she snorts. And I can't stop smiling, even when my cheeks ache.

To cap off the evening, she orders chocolate mousse for dessert, in my honor.

When the check comes, I pick up the drinks bill as promised. She insists on tipping.

I should leave it at that. A strange one-off dinner with a stranger. I should suggest never doing this again.

But instead, I hear myself say, "Same time next week?"

Her eyes widen. Then, slowly, she nods. "Yeah. Why not?"

One week becomes two. Two become months.

Every Thursday night, we claim the same table. The staff stops giving us curious looks. We stop pretending it's random.

We talk more than I expect. About her job that she

doesn't really like. About my business that often demands my attention, even at the strangest hours.

We share movies that feel like comfort food and playlists that carried us through heartbreak. She always orders pasta. I always order steak. At some stage during those weeks, we end up splitting both.

We tell ourselves it's habit. For the sake of convenience. A safe spot to lick our wounds in company.

But every Thursday, I find myself looking forward to her stories—the petty revenge fantasies she never acts on, the quiet dreams she doesn't say outright but honors in anecdotes from her childhood.

She tells me she used to play piano when she was younger. I tell her I used to play basketball before my knee gave out. She admits she still checks her ex's socials sometimes, which got more and more "cringe" over time. I confess I still sleep on the same side of the bed, even though it's empty.

There are silences too. Not awkward, but weighty. I know we're both holding back more than we should.

Eventually, she stops protesting when I pick up the bill.

She doesn't even make a clever quip when I show up one Thursday with a bouquet of roses to "match her dress." She thanks me and presses her nose to the petals, inhaling deeply with a smile on her face.

One night, she comes in late, hair damp from the rain, cheeks flushed. My chest actually aches with relief when I see her walk through the door.

"You thought I wasn't coming?" she teases.

"Maybe," I admit. "I should pick you up next time. Especially when it's raining. The traffic must be hell."

She leans in, eyes bright, voice low. "You'd miss me?"

I don't answer right away. I can't.

But the smile tugging at her mouth tells me she already knows why.

It's another rainy night when it all changes.

We're almost finished with the main course when she slides her foot against mine under the table. Not by accident.

I don't move away. Neither does she.

By the time dessert arrives, I can't taste anything but her.

I set my fork down, heart pounding. "Ash…this isn't just convenience anymore, is it?"

Her gaze doesn't waver. "No. It's not."

We leave together.

Outside, the street smells like rain. Neon bounces off puddles.

I stop under the awning, breath tight. "Ash…"

But she steps closer, fingertips brushing mine. Her eyes dare me.

So I kiss her.

It starts careful, but the way she melts against me, the way she sighs into my mouth, takes me apart without warning.

It's months of holding back breaking all at once.

When I pull back, she whispers, "Your place?"

My heart slams against my ribs. Then I grin. "Closer than mine's ever been to perfect."

We barely make it through the door.

Her laugh echoes in my living room as I pin her gently against the wall, kissing her deeper, hungrier. Her hands dig into my shirt, tugging me closer, and my palms find the softness of her waist through her red dress, her body fitting perfectly against mine. It's heat and tenderness all tangled up, every Thursday night and every almost spilling over into now.

Then I pause, my lips resting on her temple, giving her the chance to think, to breathe. Or to walk away.

"Tell me to stop, Ash."

She shakes her head. "Don't even think about it, Alvarez."

So I kiss her again, and this time it's not about filling the empty spaces.

It's about beginning something new.

The next morning, I walk into the kitchen and see her in my shirt, sitting at the counter, brows furrowed slightly as she spreads butter on slices of toast.

She looks like she owns the place.

And I know—I won't have it any other way.

"Good morning," she says, smiling when she sees me.

"Good morning," I echo.

Her smile broadens when I bring over two matching

plates from a nearby shelf. I kiss her soundly on the mouth when I set them down before her.

"Table for two, Mr. Alvarez?"

I smile back and kiss her again, certain for the first time in a long time.

"Always."

CHAPTER 9

THE WEDDING GUEST

THE FIRST TIME I SEE HER AGAIN, SHE'S WRAPPED IN ivory lace, her arm hooked around the man she chose instead of me.

It's her wedding.

And I'm a guest. Just another name on the list.

But she looks at me.

She looks at me the same way she did the night before we broke.

She looks at me like I'm the only thing she wants to run to.

The music plays. The late afternoon sun shines over the glossy white sand of the five-star resort. People clap and cheer.

The air is thick with salt—tears and sea and unspoken apologies. The wedding is by the shore, where white chairs dot the sand like bones. Her veil dances in the wind. She laughs too loudly at the best man's speech. Her mother keeps dabbing at her eyes, saying how proud she is.

I sip wine and bubbly and watch her from behind my sunglasses, the same way I always did since we were teenagers.

Only steps behind, but never close enough.

My name isn't mentioned in any speeches. It shouldn't be.

The people who do recognize me treat me with polite curiosity, discussing the weather or my trip from Manila or my latest investigative piece.

But she glances my way when she thinks no one's looking. And the way she squeezes the groom's hand like she's bracing for something tells me she still remembers everything.

The way I would buy her only baby's breath because that's all that's left in the market after work.

The long nights reading and making love.

The lazy mornings drinking coffee and watching CNN and BBC on cable.

The final fight. The ache that never stopped.

She said she needed stability, predictability. I was stories and secrets and late-night flights.

He was steady and practical; a successful architect who practically designed half the new trade zone in the outskirts of our city. The kind of man one marries.

I told her I hoped she'd be happy. She told me to never come back.

So I left.

And she waited three years to say "I do."

They slow dance under the fairy lights, in the giant

gazebo decorated with light purple and pink flowers. Her cheek rests against his.

Still, her eyes find mine over his shoulder.

She doesn't cry. She's better than that. But her lips part as if she wants to tell me something.

I nod, just once. It's an answer.

But I know it's also a goodbye.

Later, when the guests are drunk and the tide is low, I find her barefoot at the deck of the resort, staring at the moonlight pooling on the slats of wood as waves roll underneath.

"You shouldn't be here," she says, not looking up.

"I wasn't going to stay."

"Why did you come?"

"Because you sent the invitation."

"I didn't think you'd say yes."

"You wanted me to."

She turns to me then.

Her cheeks are flushed. Her makeup has smudged at the corners. Her lips are trembling.

"You left."

"You asked me to."

"I thought it would hurt less."

"Did it?"

She doesn't answer.

I take a step forward. She doesn't move.

"You look beautiful, Elsie," I say. And I mean it. God, I mean it.

"Not for you."

"No." I smile at her, hoping she sees the way I've always seen her. "But you always were."

She takes a deep breath, like she knows she might drown.

"I waited for you, Gabe."

The words leave her like ripples of foam.

She continues. It sounds like a song. "Every birthday. Every New Year. Every first rain after the summer. I waited until it made me sick."

I nod slowly. "I know."

"And you didn't come."

There's no accusation in it. Only acceptance.

"I wanted you to live. I wanted you to have what you wanted."

"I did." Her smile is so broken I almost drop to my knees. "Just not the life I needed."

Silence follows. Around us, the tide ebbs and flows. I know it will change again soon.

"I should go," I say.

She nods, but she still doesn't move.

"Tell me you don't love me, Elsie. Give me something."

She looks at me, lips parting. Then she closes her mouth tightly. Tears brim from her eyes.

"I can't."

I nod, but I feel the tears in mine too.

I let them fall. Let her see them. If she can't give me something, I will.

I pull out a tiny bundle of baby's breath from my jacket and place it by her feet.

And I leave.

It rains as I make my way to the parking lot.

The kind of rain that tastes like ash and dust.

I stand alone as it crashes down on me, ruining my good suit.

I imagine her inside, staring at her reflection in the hotel mirror, maybe holding the flowers only the two of us understand, wondering if she'll survive this choice.

I hope she does.

This is what she wanted.

And I gave it all to her.

Because some people we love so much we let them go.

Tonight, the sky tells a story of two broken hearts still beating for each other.

And I was her last story.

Even if she'll never tell that story again.

Years later, I hear from a mutual friend that her marriage didn't last.

No scandals or fights. Just a quiet, aching unraveling.

She moved to her father's hometown. She teaches English and Journalism at the university there.

She lives near the sea, keeps to herself.

Every year, on her birthday, someone leaves an unmarked bundle of baby's breath at her gate.

She never asks who. She just keeps it in a glass of water until it fades and falls apart.

Then she waits for the next one.

CHAPTER 10

DAYS OF FLOWERS

THE COLLEGE DISTRICT IS LOUD EVEN IN THE mornings.

Jeepneys honk, students spill onto sidewalks with earbuds in, tricycle and pedicab drivers yell routes. The world around me doesn't seem to stop moving.

But at *Kapehan sa Kilid*, at my corner table by the glass, it's quiet. My ritual is a cup of fresh *barako*, behind the day's newspaper I don't always read.

And the view from the window.

Always the window.

It started as habit after retirement. The doctors said to keep a routine, or I'd lose myself in the empty silence of the house. The *kapehan* became my watchpost.

Every morning, I walk from my bungalow with its garden full of aloe vera pots and *santan* beds, then I take my usual seat.

I sip the coffee they serve me without asking what I want anymore.

I breathe.

And then, one May morning, I see her.

A new flower shop, just across the street. Buckets of roses, bundles of daisies and baby's breath, white *sampaguita* glowing like pearls in the sun.

And her, tying colorful paper around stems with ribbons, brushing long black hair from her forehead with the back of her wrist.

She looks younger than me by maybe ten to fifteen years. Early forties, if I try to guess. Not married. There's no ring on her finger, as far as I can see.

She smiles at customers in a way that doesn't look forced. The students and the young professionals all love her.

I don't mean to watch. But after years of watching only shadows and exits, I find myself watching her instead.

Lila.

That's what the *kapehan*'s owner called her once, when she sent across a small bouquet of pink roses for the counter as her way of greeting her new neighbors.

The name fit perfectly.

The first time she reaches out, it startles me.

It's a white daisy, tucked into my newspaper by Roque, the young man who always brings my coffee and newspaper.

"What's this?" I ask.

He grins. "From Miss Lila, boss."

Once Roque makes his way back to the counter, I lift the flower, breathing in the softness.

When I look up, I find her already waiting, half-hidden behind a bucket of red roses.

I should look away.

Instead, I nod, pressing the daisy to my chest.

Her smile lights something in me I thought had burned out years ago.

It becomes our kind of language.

She sends *gumamela*, *sampaguita*, and roses. Roque winks at me as though he's the brains behind this entire operation.

On the fifth day, I cross the street.

"Miss Lila," I say. My voice comes out rougher than I remember. "You giving flowers to every man in the *kapehan*?"

She looks up at me, eyes amused yet assessing. She radiates an affable yet dangerously sharp air that befits a Secretary of Defense.

"Only the ones who look like they'd know how to keep them alive," she answers without hesitation.

I actually laugh. For the first time in years, it doesn't sound strange in my own throat.

"Alfred Rivero," I tell her, lowering my head slightly as I extend a hand. "Retired Army Major. At your service."

"Lila Dos Santos," she said. "Former events coordinator. HoneyBee Blossoms."

Her hand is small, but her grip is firm as she shakes mine.

I don't want to let go.

I make a habit of waiting for her in the evenings, watching as she closes up.

She sweeps petals into her dustpan, then rearranges buckets so they wouldn't topple overnight. I take her bags and walk her to her house at the end of the street. We don't even touch, but she always waves me off, watching from behind her gate as I make my way back down the narrow road.

A month later, I start waiting for her in the mornings too. I take her bags and quietly keep pace with her as she walks. I help her open the doors to her shop. I bring her coffee from across the street.

One night, she tells me that she left Manila because the cutthroat attitude of the corporate world was not for her anymore. She felt too old, too worn out.

She wanted something slower, something more real. A fresh, gentler start, just like the flowers she'd always loved.

Students and regulars whisper that the old soldier at the *kapehan* was in love with the flower lady.

Maybe they are right.

One evening, I carry something new with me.

Not a weapon, not a file, not a report. Not the only things I know how to carry.

For the first time, I carry a bouquet.

Rare blooms I asked a contact from Davao to send up: jade vine, fiery red anthurium, orchids pale as moonlight. Strange and beautiful together, tied with purple ribbons that feel like velvet to the touch.

When she finally locks up her shop and turns, I'm there.

She stares at the bouquet in surprise.

"For me?" she asks.

"For you," I answer. My voice almost fails me, but I push through. "A gift."

She touches an anthurium, almost reverently. "What are they for?"

I clear my throat. "I wanted to give you something real. Something strong. Something that endures."

I see it then. The barest hint of a smile on her lips. "And?"

I swallow the lump in my throat. I clench my stomach muscles as if anticipating a blow.

"Something that survives," I continue, "and blooms even more beautifully."

Her hand lingers on the bouquet. Her other hand slips into mine.

"Then I'll take them," she says softly. "And I'll take you."

I lean down and, at long last, kiss her.

I kiss her gently, but with certainty.

I kiss her slowly, because I had waited long enough to be sure this love can really grow.

The tricycles and pedicabs rattle by. Students spill out of stores and eateries and internet shops, laughing. The world keeps moving around us.

But for the first time in years, I feel still. Rooted.

Maybe my routine has finally found its meaning—across the street, in her arms, in this kiss that means something new is blooming.

The years blur after that, in the way only the best years do.

Every morning, I still sit by the *kapehan* window with my *barako* and newspaper.

But now there's a vase on every table too. Vases that never run empty, always filled with wild sprays of *gumamela,* white and bright daisies, or a colorful riot of roses.

And when I look up from the print, she's there.

My Lila.

Pouring sugar into her own cup, humming under her breath, her hair loose around her face, the strands now threaded through with hints of silver.

My beautiful flower lady.

My wife.

My smile and laughter after the long, hollow years of silence.

It was only during our wedding night when I found out why she sent me all those flowers in the first place.

They meant it was never too late for our kind of love to bloom.

CHAPTER 11

THE BOY AND THE SKY

I'VE PROBABLY LOOKED UP AT THE SKY A HUNDRED TIMES in the last hour.

Maybe more.

It's one of those nights where the sky feels too big, too clear. The constellations are showing off. Even the North Star shines steady and bright like it knows what it's doing.

The moon is full, a perfect white coin cut into the dark. It glows as if it's lit from within by all the fireworks and promises of the New Year.

But I can't enjoy it.

I drop my gaze back down to the street, to the sidewalk beneath my feet. The stone is cold and chipped in places. I'm sitting on a freshly painted bench at the corner of my favorite intersection, the one near the old convenience store and the ice cream shop that still plays OPM love songs from the early 2000s.

Neon signs from every direction bathe the pavement

in a chaotic kaleidoscope of red, green, yellow, orange, and blue. It should feel festive. Comforting.

It doesn't.

The pavement's stained with old gum and littered with newspapers and flyers, half-wilted in the night air. There's graffiti on the wall behind me, something angry in red spray paint I stopped trying to read twenty minutes ago.

I look up again.

And suddenly, the sky looks different.

Clouds have crept in where stars used to be. The moon's gone blurry. The blue-black canvas is turning the color of dust.

It feels like the universe is folding in on itself. Like even the stars are sick of waiting.

Like me.

I pull my legs up and rest my chin on my knees. It's been nearly two hours since I got here. Almost half a day since I said yes to Fidel's call, since I got way too excited for someone who's never even noticed me in school before.

He'd asked me to join him at the cinema. Me.

And I'd said yes so fast I could have choked on the word.

I'd dressed up—my best green sundress, the soft white cardigan I've been saving since Christmas, the pair of flats I begged my mother to buy last payday. I even raided her dresser for a touch of blush and one tiny spray of her best perfume. I looked in the mirror and thought, for once, I looked pretty.

I wanted to believe I was wanted.

And now? I'm not just alone. I'm humiliated.

He stood me up.

That scumbag Fidel stood me up.

The clock on my phone blinks mockingly. It's already 8:42 PM. He was supposed to pick me at 7:00.

I huddle deeper into my cardigan, gripping it so hard the fabric bunches at my elbows. If I had a cord in my hands, I'd wrap it around his neck and pull tight until he felt even a shred of what I feel now.

I swear, smoke's coming out of my nose.

Puff. Puff. Puff.

Damn it.

Damn him.

"Stood you up, hasn't he? Been two hours. Almost."

I jump, heart slamming against my ribcage. My body goes rigid, like I've just been caught doing something I shouldn't.

The voice comes from behind the bench.

I twist around on reflex, fists half-raised even though I've never thrown a punch in my life.

There, half-shadowed beneath the awning of the ice cream shop, is a boy. Maybe a young man. I can't really tell.

He looks like someone who doesn't belong anywhere. He's wearing a tattered hoodie and loose jeans, with a knit cap pulled low over a head of wild dark curls. He's leaning against the wall like the night belongs to him.

"Who the hell are you?" I blurt out, voice more shrill than strong.

He steps into the light and smiles—white teeth, easy grin. He looks…around my age. Maybe a little older. His eyes are deep and dark. His skin is rich brown and sun-kissed, and despite the ragged clothes, there's something solid and effortless in the way he stands.

He stands as if he knows himself. As if he's not ashamed of anything.

My goodness, he's cute. For lack of a better word.

"I'm Adam," he says, sounding like we're at a party in an expensive restaurant across the city.

I don't answer. I flop back onto the bench and cross my arms, trying not to look at him again.

But of course he slides onto the bench, right next to me.

I feel the wood groan slightly under his weight. I glance sideways. Up close, he's even more striking. There's something sharp and worldly about his features, something almost foreign. His eyes tilt up just a little at the corners, and his jawline is criminally unfair.

He's way too attractive for someone wearing a sweatshirt full of holes.

"What's your name?" he asks.

I sigh, still staring at the road. "Skye."

"Nice." He holds out a paper cup. Steam rises from the lid. "Want some? Coffee. Manang Menchie's best."

The smell wafts toward me. There's a hint of something chocolatey in it.

I usually hate when people assume I want to share space. But there's no arrogance in his offer. No smooth lines. Just…warmth.

I almost say yes.

"It smells good," I admit. "But no. Thanks, though."

He nods and sips. Silence settles between us again. Strangely, it's not awkward. Just quiet.

I peek at his clothes again. They really are too thin for this weather.

"It's freezing," I say before I can stop myself. "Aren't you cold?"

He shrugs. "I'm used to it."

His tone is soft. Not pitying. Just factual.

Then he looks at me again, and this time, there's something playful in his eyes.

"Your boy Fidel's not coming, you know."

The name hits like a slap.

My eyes narrow. "How do you know his name?"

Another shrug. "I know people. He's friends with some of the guys around here. Buys weed pretty often."

I stare at him.

No. Not Fidel.

Not Mr. MVP, Not Mr. Popularity, the golden boy of our school. He couldn't be...

Except I've heard the rumors. We all have. I just didn't want to believe them.

I open my mouth to argue, to say something cutting. But the words die in my throat.

Adam's already looking away. "You're not the first girl he's done this to. Same spot. Same move. It's almost predictable, in a way."

I blink hard, still suspended in disbelief. "You're kidding."

"I wish." He lets out a slow breath. "There was this one girl. Came back twice. The second time, she screamed at me. Thought I was stalking her and threatened to call the cops on me. All I did was try to help."

His voice cracks slightly on that last word.

I don't know what to say. The anger that's been boiling in my chest starts to soften.

We talk, slowly. Cautiously.

He tells me he left home years ago. He couldn't stand the beatings from his stepdad. Or the way his mother took her new husband's side all the time and blamed him instead.

He's been moving around ever since. Taking odd jobs. Never touching drugs. Never selling. Never running.

I believe him.

I tell him about college. About not being smart or pretty or popular to get any attention. About just being enough to get by without getting really chosen for anything.

He believes me.

It's getting late. I can feel it in my bones, in the weight of the sky pressing down.

Adam stands, stretching a little, and glances at me. "Bet they're worried about you at home."

I hesitate, then nod.

"I'll walk you," he offers. "If that's okay."

There's no pressure in his voice. Just the offer.

And something in me makes me say yes.

So I rise and fall into step beside him.

People look. Of course they do. I'm a girl in a nice dress, walking down the street with a guy who looks like he sleeps in alleys and on rooftops.

But I don't care.

Because for the first time tonight, I don't feel like someone discarded.

I feel seen.

And maybe, as we walk away from that corner under the faded lights and dying stars…

I feel like I've been chosen.

Like the real night is only just beginning.

It's two days later when I return to the bench after class.

I tell myself it's just on the way. Just a passing thought.

But the truth is, I'm hoping.

Hoping I'll see him again. Hoping I'll get to say hello. Maybe say thank you for seeing me home safely.

Maybe even buy him an ice cream, or some fishball.

But the bench is empty.

I wait for a while, pretending not to. I watch the sky again as if it might offer answers.

Then I ask around, quietly and carefully. I talk to the vendors, the old woman selling peanuts, the cigarette man with the toothy smile, even the ones lurking in the shadows of the alley.

"Adam?" I ask. "Do you know someone named Adam?"

They all shake their heads. Some don't even look up. No one knows who I'm talking about.

It's like he was never here at all.

I come back again. And again.

Even when I say I won't.

Even when I know better.

I wait through sundowns and streetlights. Through cold breezes and humid silences.

But he never comes.

I never see him again.

And yet, sometimes, when I pass by the intersection and the lights catch just right, I swear I still feel him beside me.

A ghost made of kindness.

A boy made of starlight who vanished into the city's smoke.

And maybe he was never lost.

Just passing through.

Just in time to choose me, in that one night under the glowing sky.

CHAPTER 12

LETTERS ACROSS TIME

THE DESK CAME WITH THE OLD HOUSE IN ANTIPOLO. Or maybe the house came with the desk.

It was wedged against the far wall of what looked to be the library on the ground floor, a heavy wooden thing with brass handles. Its surface bore scratches from years of pens and elbows. One drawer stuck stubbornly, as if it resented being opened.

The realtor apologized for the furniture the previous owners had left behind, but I didn't mind. I liked the idea of things carrying history.

It wasn't until I tried to tug the stubborn drawer loose that I found the box.

It was shallow, tucked in a false bottom I almost missed. Inside is a stack of envelopes tied with a piece of twine bleached pale with time.

I sat on the floor and read them all in one night.

They weren't poetic. The handwriting slanted unevenly. They were written in a combination of old-world English and Tagalog.

But they were alive. Each letter was a heartbeat, sentences about train rides and borrowed books, about waiting at stations and promises whispered between duties. About love carried like a lantern through dark years.

They were all addressed to *"My Dearest Eleanor."*

By the time I reached the last one, dated 1951, I felt like I had stolen someone's life.

And I couldn't shake the question.

What happened to them?

It wasn't hard to trace the name.

Eleanor Gatchalian had owned the house once. Records showed she'd passed away five years back, after which her son, who now lived in America, put it up for sale.

The man who wrote the letters, Lemuel Romero, had died even earlier. His return address was a modest two-story in Cainta, which the new owners had converted into a boardinghouse and *sari-sari* store.

But the woman who ran the store gave me the number of Lemuel's grandson. She said he visits once a year at least, mostly during All Souls Day, on his way to the cemetery to pay his respects to Tatay Lemuel.

I hesitate for weeks before reaching out. What do you

say to someone about a box of love letters between people who weren't even married to each other?

In the end, I send a message.

Hi. My name is Claire Norieda. I recently bought an old house in Antipolo, and in one of the furniture pieces left behind, I found something I believe belonged to your grandfather, Lemuel. Could we meet?

He replies the next morning. It's a short, direct answer. *Sure. When and where?*

We meet at a café in Quezon City, near the university where he teaches.

I expected someone older, maybe more solemn and academic-looking. Instead, Samuel Romero is in his mid-thirties, with a serious face, intense almond-shaped eyes, and dark hair that refuses to stay neat. He looks like he lives half in books, half in constant motion.

"You're Claire Norieda?" he asks as he approaches the table in the quiet corner. I picked it the moment I walked in as not too many people walk past.

"Yes." I get on my feet too quickly, nearly knocking the box of letters over. "You must be Samuel Romero."

He extends a hand. "Sam."

I take it, a little intimidated at his height and the way he's looking at me like I'm a subject he hasn't studied before. His touch is firm and warm as he shakes my hand.

He takes the chair across from mine, the box between us. I lift the lid.

"They're in chronological order," I say. "They're exactly the way I found them in the house at Antipolo."

His hands are careful as he lifts the bundle of envelopes and unties the twine.

"You're from Antipolo, then?" he asks, glancing up from the letters with a curious look.

I shake my head. "Not really, but it's my mother's hometown. She grew up there. When she retired a few years ago, she told me she wanted to live in Antipolo, to be near her sisters. That's how I found Eleanor Gatchalian's house. I guess without my father Metro Manila got a little too much for my mother."

"I'm sorry," he says softly.

"Don't be. My father's gone almost ten years now. He used to work in Ever Gotesco. I grew up in Commonwealth for the most part."

"I'm from Diliman. Second-generation professor, you can say."

"What do you teach?"

"Undergrad History."

I smile, nodding toward the letters in his hands. "These are perfect for you, then. Real pieces of history."

The café noise seems to settle as Sam begins to read. His mouth tightens at some lines, softens at others. When he sets the paper down after nearly an hour, his thumb lingers on the faded ink.

"These were his," he says quietly. "I've only heard about them. I didn't think they'd survived. But I'd know his handwriting anywhere."

"You…knew? About them?"

"Lolo used to tell me stories," he says. "About a

beautiful girl whom he loved enough to write every week, even when he had nothing. Even when distance and war kept them apart. That girl was Eleanor."

I swallow hard at the revelation. "Do you know…what happened between them?"

He hesitates before answering. "Eleanor married someone else. Lolo married someone else, too, but it didn't last long. Lola died soon after giving birth to my father. She was a very delicate woman. I have a few pictures of her that I got from Lolo. Eleanor was… someone before. Lolo's first love."

The air changes, heavier with a sadness I didn't expect.

Sam exhales, eyes fixed on the table as he continues. "They loved each other since they were very young. Everyone thought they'd marry. But he was drafted. She waited two years, then her parents arranged a match with another family, wealthier than Lolo's. By the time Lemuel came home, she was already promised. It was too late. Breaking engagements in the old days brought dishonor to the entire family."

My throat tightens. "So they loved each other."

"Yes," he says simply. "But love wasn't enough then."

That should have been the end of it.

But Sam asks if I'd like to help him go through the letters.

"Some of the handwriting's hard to read," he admits. "And I think…their story deserves to be remembered properly. Transcribing the letters electronically would be a good idea. If you've got the time, of course."

We begin meeting every Sunday at the same café.

The first Sunday, I read aloud. Lemuel's words fill the café like echoes from another time.

"My dearest Eleanor, if I could fold the miles between us into this page, I would never let you be lonely again."

I feel heat rise in my chest, though it wasn't me he was writing to.

The second Sunday, we argue.

"Look at this one," Sam says. "He promises her forever, but he had no way to guarantee anything. Isn't that reckless?"

"It's not reckless," I shoot back. "It's brave. Words were all he had."

He laughs at how fierce I sound, then softens. "You'd have believed him, wouldn't you?"

"Yes," I answer haughtily.

"Lolo would have really adored you," he says.

That makes me blush.

The third Sunday, we slip into ease.

Sam volunteers to pick me up from my house in Commonwealth, then rolls into our neighborhood in a silver-black Yamaha.

I don't comment. I only take the helmet he offers me.

At the café, he tells me about his students, who are mostly freshmen and sophomores. I tell him about working for various international schools in the UAE for more than a decade, then coming back home to open my own little preschool and daycare so I could take care of my mother.

Between sips of coffee, we return to the letters.

Another fragment stands out, making us pause.

"Even if the world changes its mind about us, know that I will not change my own. My heart has no other home but you."

My voice falters when I read it. Sam doesn't ask why.

By the fourth Sunday, it's no longer just about Eleanor and Samuel.

"Do you ever think we only find things because we're meant to?" I ask as we pack the letters back into the box.

Sam's hand brushes mine when he hands me the twine.

"Lately," he answers quietly.

When he drops me off at my house, I lean in and kiss his cheek before going inside.

When we reach the final envelope, dated the 14th of February 1951, the café seems hushed, as though it knows.

The handwriting is shaky by then. The letter itself is short.

I hope you are happy, Eleanor.

If he is kind, then I am at peace.

I do not regret loving you. I never will.

I set the page down, my chest aching, my eyes prickling.

"That's it."

Sam nods.

"That's it," he echoes. "A few years later, Lolo met Lola. Then they got married soon after."

"It feels unfair," I whisper.

"Most real stories are," he says. "History is a collection of all that."

I turn to him. "But they loved each other, didn't they? They deserved more."

He's silent for a long time. Then he says, "Maybe their ending isn't ours to fix. But maybe it's a reminder. That sometimes love doesn't survive time. And sometimes…it waits for someone else to carry it forward."

His words hang between us like a fragile bridge.

But when he drops me off, he's the one who kisses me.

A quick peck on the lips.

I don't kiss him back.

That night, I hug the box of letters to my chest and cry myself to sleep.

The next Sunday, Sam comes to my door and rings the bell.

When I open the gate, I see him standing on the pavement in his motorcycle jacket, helmet in one hand, a small maroon envelope in the other.

Without a word, he extends the envelope to me. My name's written on it in bold black marker.

"What's this?" I ask, somewhere between curiosity, surprise, and anxiety.

"Read it," he says. "Please."

I lift the flap and unfold the letter tucked inside. It's handwritten on yellow ruled paper.

My dearest Claire,

I don't know if people still write letters the way Lolo did. Maybe the world moves too fast now. But I've been spending these Sundays with you, and I felt I couldn't let the story of Eleanor and Lemuel go just yet.

Then I realized that it wasn't them I couldn't let go of.

It was you.

So here is my story.

I look forward to Sundays because they mean you. Because visiting the past doesn't feel lonely when you're across the table. Because when I read his words with you, I'm reminded that love isn't only a memory or a part of history.

It's a possibility, here and now.

If Lemuel could write Eleanor every week, then let this be my first letter to you. I hope there will be more.

Yours,

Samuel

My eyes blur before I even reach the end. I lower the page slowly, afraid to breathe too loudly.

He's watching me nervously, vulnerable in a way I hadn't seen before.

"I didn't want Lemuel and Eleanor's story to be the only one that we share," he says softly.

I press my hand over the letter, over my name.

"Thank you," I murmur, reaching out to touch his hand.

He turns his palm so our fingers could tangle.

And when he leans across the space between us, he kisses me.

And I kiss him right back.

It's not rushed. It's not hesitant.

It's just certain.

And it tastes like a beginning, not an ending.

I had the desk moved from Antipolo to the house in Commonwealth.

Now, it rests in a place of honor at the corner of my home office. I always make sure there's a vase of fresh flowers on it, next to a framed photograph of Lemuel taken in the early 1940s. In it, he's dressed in a dark American suit, hair slicked back from his serious face with those familiar intense eyes. He's looking away from the camera, maybe toward his love.

The false drawer is empty now, except for two envelopes.

One with Eleanor's name. Lemuel's first letter.

And one with mine. Sam's first letter.

The rest of his Lolo's letters live with Sam now, catalogued and safely kept. Sometimes he shows them to his students, teaching them that history isn't only about wars and treaties, but also about real people.

People who loved, who lost, who left behind paper hearts for strangers to find.

People whose stories never really ended.

Because what I found that night in the desk wasn't the end of Lemuel and Eleanor's love story.

It was the beginning of ours.

ABOUT THE AUTHOR

Shirley Siaton writes edgy and evocative novels and poems. Her worlds are in a deliciously dark cross-section of the romance, neo-noir, action, contemporary, and fantasy genres. Her background in various Asian martial arts inspires a lot of her work.

She has several books of fiction and poetry released since February 2023. Her first book is the free verse collection *Black Cat and other poems*. *Befallen* (March 2025) is her first full-length novel. She also pens juvenile literature as Shirley Parabia.

She is an award-winning writer, poet, and journalist in English, Filipino, and Hiligaynon. Her essays, short stories, and poems have been published internationally in print and digital media. Her multi-lingual plays have been staged in the Philippines.

Shirley is a black belt in Shotokan Karate and an international certified fitness coach. She has a Master's degree in Public Administration and works in education, wellness, and publishing. Originally from Iloilo City, she lives in the Middle East with her husband and two daughters.

ON THE WEB

Shirley's official website:
shirleysiaton.com

Complete reading guide:
shirley.pub

Subscribe to Shirley's VIP list for free exclusive updates:
newsletter.shirleysiaton.com